THE MONEY TREE

THE MONEY TREE

SARAH STEWART

Illustrations by DAVID SMALL

FARRAR · STRAUS · GIROUX / *New York*

For Edwin and Mary

In January, when Miss McGillicuddy was making a quilt in front of the fire, she noticed an unusual shape outside her living-room window.

In February, as Miss
McGillicuddy was looking
up from her book, she
realized that the new shape
was a small tree. "A gift
from the birds," she said to
herself.

In March, while Miss
McGillicuddy was flying
her favorite kite, its tail
got caught in a limb of
the new tree. "What a
strange shape," she
thought as she tugged.

In April, when Miss McGillicuddy was planting snow peas, she paused and stared at the tree, now covered in the fresh green colors of spring. "How odd," she mused, "that it has grown so very large in such a short time."

In May, as Miss McGillicuddy was making a Maypole for the neighborhood children, she realized, to her great surprise, that the leaves on the tree were not leaf-shaped at all! Being careful not to hurt the tender branches, she gave each child some of the tree's crisp green foliage as a party favor.

In June, while Miss McGillicuddy was gathering a bouquet of roses, parents of the neighborhood children appeared in the yard. When they said they had come to see the strange tree, she invited them to take home a few cuttings.

In July, when Miss McGillicuddy was picking cherries in her orchard, the town officials asked if they could use some of the greenery for special projects. She let them borrow her ladder—the tree was growing larger every day—and went inside to make cherry cobbler.

In August, as Miss McGillicuddy was returning home, she noticed that most of the people carrying bags and baskets away from the tree were perfect strangers! "No matter," she said, "the branches would break from their burden if someone was not picking all the time."

Jefferson Elementary School
1538 N. 15th Street
Sheboygan, WI 53081

In September, while Miss McGillicuddy was feeding the animals, she watched the crowd around the tree surging back and forth beneath the harvest moon. "Don't they ever rest?" she asked herself.

In October, when Miss
McGillicuddy was making
faces on her pumpkins, she
realized that the leaves on
the tree were turning yellow
and brown. She sighed
with relief.

In November, as the first
winter storm arrived, Miss
McGillicuddy watched
a few determined strangers
scratching at the snow under
the tree.

In December, Miss McGillicuddy and the neighbor boys cut down the tree. Although the wood was green and certain to smoke a little, she didn't mind, for now she had enough to keep warm through the coldest winter.

Miss McGillicuddy gave each boy a loaf of homemade bread, a jar of strawberry jam, and a bouquet of dried flowers. Then she said goodbye, walked toward the warmth of the fire, and smiled to herself.